The Adventures of

Annie and

Svetlana Kosakov

Antonio Garcia Jr.

AuthorHouse™
1663 Liberty Drive
Bloomington, IN 47403
www.authorhouse.com
Phone: 1 (800) 839-8640

Published by AuthorHouse

ISBN: 978-1-5246-4353-9 (sc)
ISBN: 978-1-5246-4354-6 (e)

Library of Congress Control Number: 2016916548

Print information available on the last page.

authorHOUSE®

The Adventures of Annie and Svetlana Kosakov

The 12 Masks of Colcocan

By Antonio Garcia Jr

The quest in the search of the lost city of Colcocan and the legend of the twelve masks that activates an ancient telescope that searches the stars based on their ancient Mayan calendar, but it also hides an ancient secret of a hidden Mayan city in an another dimension hidden in the Island of Kolcan. An island that no one knows until now.

An Introduction:

The Characters:

For Annie and her sister Svetlana Kosakov along with their brothers and their cousins the Vlascos and their archeologist friends; as they embark to a journey in search of the 12 masks of Colcocan and the quest to find it before a notorious villain and a British rogue archeologist claim jumper try to put all the stops on the group from reaching the mask. So come on and get a safari helmet or an Indy hat and a bomber jacket, and join in on an adventure that will take you to the Mayan regions of Mexico and Belize; so on with the adventure! And now we introduce you to all the characters from heroes to villains:

Annie Kosakov:

Age: 18

Heights: 6'2"

Weight: 115 lbs.

Siblings: Andy (brother) – Gregory (Brother) – Svetlana (sister).

Hair Color: Blonde

Eyes color: Light blue

Annie Kosakov is the eldest of the Kosakov brothers and sisters. She was born in Houston, TX from a Russian Naval Admiral and an American Navy Commander officer. She is very smart and cunning and an expert archeologist mainly on the Mayan Civilization where she and her young sister go to Mexico and Belize to explore the Mayan Ruins. She is very athletic; an expert in martial arts with very powerful and lethal and an excellent swimmer when trying to find lost objects that has archeological value, Annie is a very cook expert; especially in Mayan and Yucatecan culinary dishes.

Annie's apparel consists in a safari helmet, a short sleeve lemon green safari jacket with double pocket s and an olive green belt with an antique gold belt buckle a short sleeve khaki shirt, white slim fit jeans with a green olive web belt with an antique gold belt buckle, brown boots, along with brown gloves. She also has blonde yellow long hair with light blue eyes and a pair of white marble earrings.

Svetlana Kosakov:

Age: 17

Heights: 5'7"

Weight: 95 Lbs.

Siblings: Andy (brother) - Gregory (brother) - Annie-(sister)

Hair Color: Red Orange

Eyes Color: Green Blue

Svetlana Kosakov is the youngest sister of the Kosakov Brothers and Annie's youngest sister. She was born in Moscow, Russia from a Russian Navy Admiral and an American Naval Commander which they have a strong family relationship when they come from an international military family with strong ties with their cousins and their relatives who all live in Houston, TX. Like her sister; Svetlana is a very adventurous teenage girl who likes to go on a quest for a lost civilization like the Mayans and is an expert in archeology especially in the Mayan culture, she is also an expert diver and a very fast swimmer and excellent fighter in martial arts even she is excellent in fighting underwater combat. Svetlana is also an excellent cook and a good story teller about her adventures while babysitting which is her way of income in order to save and buy an suv and a military off road truck. Like her sister, Svetlana has an orange hair with a large curved tuff with three small curved tuffs and her apparel consist an aqua green safari helmet with an ocean blue head band, a khaki short sleeve polo shirt a short sleeve aqua green safari jacket with an ocean blue belt with an antique gold belt buckle and golden brown gloves, she also wears white slim fit jeans with a white web belt with an antique gold belt buckle and a pair of desert sand boots with a zipper on the sides.

Svetlana wears a pair of white marble earrings on her ears and brown tan gloves when she goes on an archeological expedition in the Mayan region when she's handling archeological artifacts. Like Annie; Svetlana is a good swimmer and she is not afraid to get her clothes wet when they are diving underwater on her safari apparel with her air tanks. Svetlana also likes to babysit in order to get extra money for the things she needs for a next adventure. Now that we have the main characters we introduce the other characters and their relatives of the Korsakov's.

Dwayne Vlasco:

Age: 12

Height: 4' 7"

Weight: 75 Lbs.

Sibling Emily, sister

Hair Color: Brown

Eyes color: Brown

Dwayne Vlasco is the younger brother of Emily Vlasco and an important part of the Vlasco detective team whose cousins are part of the team. With good sense of humor and an adventure spirit, Dwayne springs up to action to help the team when they are ever in danger, he's there to get them out of the jam and put the bad guy away and helping them solve the mystery.

Dwayne is an expert in cracking codes and encryptions and excellent computer programmer when operating the most advance computer. Dwayne's apparel consists of a blue tee with a flame on the front with stripes on the sort sleeves, a gray beret with a white fur ball on the top front, he also wears purple pants, but when on safari or when he goes fishing; he wears white skinny jeans, he also wears white socks and blue and white stripe athletic shoes with black stripes on the sides from front to back.

Emily Vlasco:

Age: 17

Height: 5'8"

Weight: 85 lbs.

Sibling: Dwayne(brother)

Hair Color: Mid tone orange

Eyes Color: Aqua blue wears glasses

Emily Vlasco is the elder sibling and is the daughter of the famous Texas private detective Tony Vlasco and works as her secretary and her assistant in helping her father on some certain cases. She is also nice, but she can be very strict when she's in charge, she is also a senior Bluebonnet Guide officer who is in charge and her cousin Cathy Vlasco who is also a junior Bluebonnet Guide is on command of the Bluebonnet girl's troop 77504 based in Pasadena, TX and Deer Park, TX.

Emily's apparel consists of her Bluebonnet uniform consisting in a white cowboy Stetson gambler hat with short top, a white polo shirt, a light blue sweater vest, with a yellow sash with a lot of merit patches on it, she also wears a blue miniskirt with a white belt around it and blue and red stripe shoes with white socks. Her casual apparel consists only a white shirt short sleeve with a pink sweater vest with a pink lavender neck scarf around her neck, along with a red mini skirt with a white belt around her and white stretch high cuff go-go boots mid heel. And last her jungle and safari apparel consist in a safari cowboy hat with the left flap folded, she wears a short sleeve pilot shirt with double pockets along with olive green cargo shorts with a belt, socks and a light tan brown rider boots with tread soles and tread sole heels as well. She also wears white slim fit jeans with a khaki shirt, a gray shirt or a lemon green shirt as part of her jungle apparel including white go-go boots and brown rider's boots. She is very athletic, fast runner and a very fast swimmer and a very lethal martial artist who also is a very good boxer and a wrestler. Emily is also a member of the NASA Space summer camp astronauts who participates in space projects along with her brother Dwayne who participate in space walks and moon walks along with their cousins.

Cathy Vlasco:

Age: 14

Height: 5'6"

Weight 88 Lbs.

Sibling: Eddy "Guy" Vlasco (brother)

Hair color: Red Terracota.

Eyes: Light Blue, Cathy also wears eye glasses.

Cathy is the younger sister of Eddy "Guy" Vlasco and sometimes both participate in their cousins detective adventures on solving mysteries. She also is great in math and loves archeology and space where she is member of the NASA Space summer camp where she is now practicing spacewalks and moonwalks where she has a modified compacted spacesuit, a generator backpack which includes two air tanks and a auxiliary mask with an air hose attached to her air tank in case her space helmet is pulled off or has been ejected by accident. She's an excellent swimmer and is not afraid to get her Blubonnet girl uniform or her clothes with her white boots and her white winter jacket all wet, although she likes to stay in the swimming pool where the tempature is always right. She is a junior Bluebonnet guide who has the highest number of patches that she has ever earned and has become the troop leader of Troop 77504 since she was in fifth grade. Cathy's apparel in her Blubonnet uniform which consist on a stetson gambler cowboy hat with a short top, a white polo shirt with a pocket and her vest is light blue along with a gold sash with patches along with a navy blue miniskirt with a white belt, she also wears white tall socks with white gloss Mary Jane shoes or white tall cuff boots she also wears slim fit white jeans. She also wears a short sleeve pocket shirt with a pink sweater vest along with a red miniskirt with a white belt along with white high cuff go-go stretch boots during the summer, in the winter she wears a pink turtle neck shirt along with a red vest and a a white sweater and a white goose feather belt jacket with red and pink shoulder stripes on the top front and back along with blue jeans with white socks and her white go-go stretch mid heel boots. Cathy also wears a light aqua blue tee with white slim fit jeans with a white web belt and white canvas boat shoes.

Cathy is very athletic in sports and is great fighter with a powerful jab and hook, to martial arts with a blackbelt 10th degree level, the highest, but she can be vulnerable by distraction and could be subdued by zapping her with a stun ray gun or by a tranquilizer dart. She also has the highest IQ and is the smartest girl of the Vlasco clan when trying to resolve mystery cases. So if you try to outsmart Cathy, think again; she could outsmart you.

Cathy Vlasco

Eddy "Guy" Vlasco

Age: 16

Height: 5' 7"

Weight: 118lbs

Sibling: Cathy Vlasco (sister)

Hair color: Dark brown

He is known as the cool kid from Deer Park and the greatest junior private eye of the park. When there's a mystery; Eddy is there to solve the caper. When he's in tough situation to solve a mystery or trying to figure out a clue, he'll ask his little sister to help him on the case. Eddy is also a very athletic kid who likes sports mainly fooball, basketball and baseball and he's under a crush from a pretty girl who is a cheerleader. Eddy also likes to cook like his mother and father who own a pub restaurant named O' Flahertys where he and his sister and their cousins and their uncles and aunts play Irish music on Friday and Saturday which is Irish music weekend band contest where there are great prizes to win. Eddy knows how to fight and wrestle bullies and thugs when his little sister is in trouble and will defend her if she's surrounded by bullies and thugs who may try to steal her fundraiser money for the Bluebonnet Girls cookie and pastry sales and he will never do a dirty stint on her sister because he cares about her and repects her so much and his future girlfriend. Eddy's apparel is more summerlike than all the characters mentioned, Eddy wears a fedora hat, but when they go to a jungle adventure; he wears an Indiana Jones hat when he's on an adventure with his cousins. He also wears an aquagreen short sleeve jacket along with a black t-shirt with a black skull in the front, he wears brown pants with white short socks with green and dark green athletic white stripes on both sides.

And now we will introduce the other characters in this archeological adventure in the Ribera Maya of the State of Quintana Roo in Mexico and the country of Belize in an island for the quest and search for the mask of Colcocan.

Professor Monica Delgado Foster:

Archeologist and Director of the Mayan Museum of Culture and Archeological Institute located in Chetumal Quintana Roo Mexico, is in charge of the Colcocan expedition in the search of the mask and the instruction scroll in order to activate the mask. She is married to the famous surfer and TV realty adventurer Sidney "jalapeño" Foster who is now a Mexican citizen and helps Professor Delgado on any expidition and has twins, a son and a daughter who too they love adventures.

Sidney "Sid " "jalapeño" Foster:

If you hear this catchphrase when ever he's hungry for danger, he get's it for breakfast, danger for lunch and danger for dinner; then your referring to Sid "jalapeño" Foster who loves to eat jalapeño peppers for breakfast, lunch and dinner and a occassional snack. A famed championed surfer, Sid is not only an adventurer, he loves danger and the close encounter in fighting and taking down a big saltwater crocodile, or a big boa constrictor and having a big fight to the death with an anaconda which the snake always ends up being in boots, belts and wallets thanks to Sid's killer punch breaking the snakes jaw sending him to the taxidermist. Despite his Aussie accent, Sid was born in Orange Walk, Belize (now a Mexican Citizen) from an Australian father and a Belizean mother, he met a Mexican archeologist Professor Monica Delgado when he started working with her on archeological expeditions in the Mayan Region in the state of Chiapas in Mexico until she was hired by the State government of Quintana Roo to become director of the Museum and Archeological Institute. Sid loves his kids that they are both following their parents footsteps in pursuing their lifetime careers.

Cody Manuel Foster:

He looks a little bit like his dad, but Cody is the older twin brother by five minutes and looks a little bit by his sister whose five minutes younger. He is also a high grade student with scores and very athletic in sports

Xochil Beth Foster:

Xochil Beth is the younger twin sister who is five minutes younger that her twin brother who are good in sports and in math. She is a good archeologist and want's to follow her mom's footsteps. Like her brother, Xochil is a great fighter and knows how to take down any culprit when ever she's threaten. She loves to cook and makes the best pina colada ever (non alcoholic).

So get your camp equipment ready, your passport, wardrobe and your favorite food and snacks and drinks as we travel to the Yucatan Peninsula as we explore the world of the Mayan Civilization in the quest for the Mask of Colcocan.

The 12 Masks of Colcocan

Chapter 1:

Ah the Rivera Maya is the best place to have a good vacation all year long including in the hurricane season.

But there is also a dark past when claim jumpers, tomb raiders and bandits looted and robbed in the pyramids temples from the Mayan ruins ancient objects and sacred scrolls to sell them in the black market to the highest bidder to any museum for any exhibition to make millions in assets or to make future expeditions in finding and looting more ancient Mayan cities where the kings and chieftains had more treasures to be stolen than being studied on the history of the artifact or the ancient scroll that tells the history when it was founded and when it was abandoned that they will never know how the ancient cities and villages have existed, until now when in the city of Cancun on the summer home of the retired Russian Navy Adm. Dimitri Kosakov and his wife retired US Navy Captain Betty Thomason-Kosakov who are now living in Seabrook, TX where they own and run a naval academy which is also their home for their family of two sons and two daughters now growing up. Back at the summer house Annie and her sister Svetlana were getting their camping and expedition gear ready to load up in their two six by six Yuri trucks as they were waiting for their cousins to finish up packing and getting ready for their first expedition in the quest for the mask of Colcocan in the island of Kolcan which is located fifteen miles of the coast of Thompson Beach, Belize in the Caribbean sea in a small bay called Copal Bay and it's the most pristine and transparent bay in al Belize.

Come on guys, we got to put all the camping gear, the canoes, live vest, rafts and all the archeological equipment in both trucks. Cathy

Don`t forget the food and water and the stove and the portable cooler.

Svetlana:

And don't forget taking your duffle bag and your toiletries with you, the last time you left them in your room we have to come back and get them.

Cathy

Sorry.

As everyone had finished packing and loading the two trucks and hitching the trailer boats on the schedule, not far from there in a vast mansion has a view from the Cancun hotel area that next to the beach.

There's a multi-millionaire whose business is the crime business that runs from piracy to looting archeological objects, smuggling to loan sharking by extortion and bribing local government to law enforcement officials, Constantino Bosco is known to run the criminal business with finesse especially in archeological artifacts to sell the highest collector in an anonymous bidder in the ancient artifacts black market. Known to the underground crime as Don Bosco, he and his henchmen have often control the wharf where he controls the tourist industry where he dupes his victims by going to their hotel they are conned by the hidden high fees he imposes on different activities from sail fishing to archeological tourist expeditions where he gets a high percentage of the commissions and kick-backs from his fraudulent schemes.

But he has two of his henchmen who do all the dirty work for him in a very goofy way, Gabino Estanislao Vasco alias "Gatula"" and Eulalio Tamez alias "El Regio", and there not your classic goons but two dopey and dumbest criminals that always screw up any job that their boss always tells them which ends up screwing the whole operation making them by getting their ears yanked with the threat of getting contracts over their heads.

But there's another player who is also looking for the mask of Colcocan only to sell it to the highest bidder of any famous museum in Europe but in the whole wide world, and for any curator and any museum director will have to pay millions of Euros extra to the most evasive archeologist and very mysterious and dangerous woman of all referring to Laura Craftshire, the most infamous tomb raider and rogue archeologist with the help of her assistant Heather Leafshire; these two ladies have gone and retrieved more ancient artifacts in raiding tombs and chambers and selling the spoils to any collectionist in a very but secretive meeting with one who was doing the highest bidding lost to Laura was none other her nemesis than Don Bosco who vowed to eliminate her and her assistant if they try to take the mask.

Back at the summer home; everybody was excited after they got all their gear and other things at the truck as they were getting ready to ride all the way to Chetumal to reunite with Professor Monica Delgado-Foster and her kids who they want to explore the Mayan ruins of Colcocan in the search of the mask and the scroll.

Meanwhile back on the road Annie was explaining to Guy and his sister Cathy about the search for the mask and what it means to her in helping Professor Delgado-Foster for the future project of restoring the city of Colcocan and the lost Mayan culture and its history since it was conquered and ransacked by the Spanish in 1525 according to the only record that the museum had and it was determined to save and preserve the most important artifacts and scrolls which chronicles the history of Colcocan. According to the history of the city, Colcocan was founded in a cenote which also serves as a refuge when a hurricane used to make a landfall heading towards the mainland.

Guy

So you think that the city of Colcocan was founded in a cenote before it expanded right outside the on the edges of the cenote right?

Cathy:

According to the legend that the Mayans were advance engineers and built the first aqueducts that supplied clean freshwater to the certain villages and to the port around the island.

Annie:

What might be on that question that we don't know when what year it was founded and Cathy's comment that the Mayans were advance engineers in building the first aqueducts supplying fresh water to the villages and to the main port is correct, they were the first to create math and other calculations that created and built this city before the Spanish conquistadors captured it and turned the city into a military fortress to defend and deter any pirate activity. And by the way; here's a picture of Kolcan Island next to Copal Island where there's a village and a lagoon where legend says that the mask is hidden in the lagoon and the scroll is hidden in the bottom of the cenote, Professor Foster will let us know where the scroll is since there are caverns that go through the surface.

By seeing the photograph, looking for the mask and the scroll was trying to find the needle in the haystack and this was no needle in the haystack and they have to find the mask which was protected by booby-traps and rumors say that there was a giant octopus hiding in the lagoon guarding and will kill and eat any intruder that tries to take the mask out of the cavern.

This was one thing that they have to be careful when they run on certain kind of booby-traps they might encounter when they try to find the mask and the scrolls.

It was almost night time when the two trucks with their trailers have just arrived at Chetumal where they arrived at the Mayan Museum of Archeological and Cultural Institute of The State of Quintana Roo where they arrived to meet Professor Monica Delgado-Foster who was getting all the information and maps that lead to the islands, there the parties have just entered the museum towards her office where all the papers and maps and some books were mentioning the history of the Mayas and it's extension of the kingdom from the Yucatan Peninsula to the Gulf of Tehuantepec to the Southern region of Guatemala, Belize to the Southeast region of Honduras and El Salvador. Later that night Professor Delgado-Foster invited their guest to spend at least two days while the Professor finishes packing and get the proper papers and passports to go to Belize, there the group will go all together to Thompson Beach where they'll meet Professor Delgado-Foster's husband and well known adventurer Sid Foster aka Jalapeno the adventurer and five time surfer champion who knows how to shave and tame those wild waves, whenever someone ask what's his favorite food, he says that danger is his favorite food for breakfast, lunch and dinner, but he carries a small plastic bag of fresh hot jalapenos as a snack when he's on an adventure, he also like to wrestle gators and crocs as well an anaconda or two just to build up more muscle to pack up more punch.

While they are talking and packing; outside the museum not far in a two story apartment were two men with an apparent mobster attitude acting like goons doing their bosses dirty work which they screw up all the time getting their boss angry in a tight up situation when they make their narrow escape from being captured by the cops and federales and from the US armed forces mainly from the Navy Seals.

Gatula:

Hey Regio look out there, I see two trucks with travel trailers attached and there are some kids with the professor; looks like they are planning to go to the island of Kolcan in search of the mask of Colcocan.

Regio:

You got to be kidding, the professor with a bunch of kids going to Kolcan Island in search of the mask.

Gatula:

No I`m not, hey! I saw that girl in a local paper back in Houston; she's the girl who won a contest on archeology studying the Mayan Culture and was invited along with their other cousins. We better tell the boss right away before they leave, Regio, Regio where are you?

But they were not alone because there were two more who were watching and eaves' dropping about two houses from the museum and from Sid's house was Laura Craftshire and her side kick and assistant Heather Leafshire who were one step ahead of Don Bosco.

Heather:

When do we get our hands on that map that will lead us to that mask?

Laura:

Patience Heather; it's too risky to go in and get the map out of them, besides we need to stay away from the lime light of Interpol and Europol; they might have an agent at our tails and we don`t want to reveal ourselves and getting exposed.

Heather:

What about the crime boss "Don Bosco"; he might be after the mask and probably he might have put contracts on our lives and heads.

Laura:

That's one thing that we have taken the risk before with other rivals and nemesis but not with "Don Bosco". We'll have to deal with him sooner or later.

Meanwhile back at the residence; the two goons were spying or only one was keeping an eye on the archeologist and her helpers while the other goon was eyeing on pretty ladies especially talking to an American blonde when Gabino aka Gatula saw him flirting with the pretty blonde lady until he had to go out the door and grab him by the ear and yanking him back to the house not before Eulalio gave the lady his cellphone number.

Gatula:

What are you doing you moron! What were you thinking! Don`t you know that American lady could be an agent from the CIA, Naval Intelligence, DEA, FBI or from Interpol.

Regio:

Vamos Estanislao, you don't have to be a paranoid because I like to see a pretty lady.

Gatula:

You don`t understand, you want us to get arrested and thrown in to the "big house"?

Regio:

Ah no.

Gatula:

Good; let's call "Don Bosco" and tell them about the professor and her helpers that they are about to leave Chetumal to Kolcan Island.

Laura Craftshire and Heather Leafshire

Chapter: 2

It was morning when the Professor and her kids were making breakfast as Annie was getting ready to pack up the last camp gear before they head towards the border crossing in Belize and a long four hours' trip towards Thompson Beach near the Honduran border for a long sail to Kolcan Island in search of the mask of Colcocan where if might be hidden in the bottom of the cavern in the South side of the island but in the island of Copal as well. After that, they all left for Belize after they crossed the border and waiting for fifteen minutes to get the clearance before heading to Thompson Beach before night fall, but they were not going alone because not far was an suv with two British women heading towards the same destination but by boat with a different plan to follow them when they find the mask and steal it and sell it to the highest bidder to any curator of any British or European museum or any private collector who has the millions to spend.

But they were not only ones who were looking for the mask, Constantino Bosco aka "Don Bosco" and his two goons were sailing in his multi luxury yacht called "La Tintorera" or "The Inker" were directly sailing towards

Copal and Colcocan Island to get their hands on that mask before Professor Craftshire and her sidekick get their hands on that mask as they were navigating the famous coral reefs that makes Belize a famous tourist attraction for scuba diving and other aquatic sports, as they were heading towards Belize City to buy camping and underwater gear.

Not far, another boat was heading towards Belize City to pick up supplies and dive gear for sport fishing purposes which was a cover up to avoid any suspicious activity relating to mask of Colcocan that would alert the Belizean authorities.

Laura:
Looks like "Don Bosco" has got ahead of us by docking his boat to get supplies and other gear.

Heather:
It looks like diving gear and spear guns; he's a heavy hitter on his league in his own pride. We better get our equipment, the sooner the better.

Laura:
We already have Heather and we will dock at The South Belizean Yacht club to get the diving equipment, wet suits and a metal detector so we can find the mask and other relics for keeps.

Heather:
We can beat him in his own game.

Laura:
Indeed it is. He'll squirm like a worm when we have the mask and any other artifact.

Don Bosco:
So there are other competitors in looking for that mask, well the place is so crowded that we'll have to start eliminating the competition so there will one and that's me.

Gatula:
But "Don Bosco" how where going to eliminate them, there too many including kids and that British tomb raider and her companion, they might be getting ahead of us before reaching Kolcan Island.

Don Bosco:
What did I tell you before; we will go to the island first follow them take the mask and dump them to the bottom of the sea with cement blocks tied to ropes so they don`t float! Any questions before I send somebody to Davy Jones Locker?

Both goons:
Ah no.

Don Bosco:
Then it's settled; now let's leave the port before that tomb raider tries to leave first.

Both:
Yes Sir.

But it was too late; Laura and her sidekick Heather were already ahead of them with a three hours' advantage making "Don Bosco" so furious that he wanted to settle the score with Laura since he got ripped off on an expedition in search of the tomb of a Mayan Chieftain on a small village which Laura and "Don Bosco" discovered six years ago.

"Don Bosco and his henchmen wanted to take the mask and sell it to the highest bidder in the Yucatan Peninsula and keep the whole money to himself, that's when Laura swipe the mask from him and started to run not before that she had to knock out the two henchmen and dodging bullets from Don Bosco before being hit by a dart gun which the dart contained snake venom from an area around Quintana Roo where the ruins of the same small Mayan village that she discovered three years back and met her sidekick Heather Leafshire who had and antidote which saved her life and in return both women started to work together in the claim jumping business.

Chapter: 3

After spending the day in Belize City; Annie, Svetlana along with the crew started to drive towards Thompson Beach to meet Professor Delgado-Foster's husband to spend the night and plan to sail towards Kolcan Island in search of the Mask of Colcocan and the ancient scroll, though they never plan to sail from Cancun to Chetumal and to sail towards Kolcan Island, they decide to travel by road to Chetumal to meet Professor Monica Delgado-Foster and her two children so they could join and travel on a road trip to Thompson Beach, Belize before night fall where Professor Delgado-Foster will meet her husband Sid '' jalapeño" Foster and all will head towards Copal and Kolcan Island where the group will split in two to explore

At Kolcan Island "Don Bosco's" luxury yacht "La Tintorera" has anchored at the Northeast side of the island where no one will suspect that he's in the island looking for the mask, then a second yacht came only to anchor in Copal Island and it was the "English Beauty" own by Laura Craftshire as she was preparing to explore the island the next morning along with her sidekick Heather Leafshire were preparing to dive underwater near the cavern in the shallow lagoon where rumors say that a giant man-eating octopus lives in that cavern and has been lurking in and out of the lagoon and in to the sea in search of food which has been eating sharks some other fish and crustaceans but no humans after the last habitants of Copal Island have left for Kolcan Island after the last pure Mayan maiden was sacrificed as an offer for rain so the crops will grow for the autumn harvest.

Lucky it was a Mayan tale to scare off any looter who would try to steal any golden or silver artifacts if they try to cross the lagoon by boat where the octopus might drag them down to the bottom of the sea and into a cavern where they are eaten and the skeletons are lying all over the ocean floor. Later that night, Annie and her group had just arrived at Thompson Beach where they Professor Delgado-Foster husband Sid where her kids gave him the hugs and kisses as they arrived as Sid greeted his guest as they were guided to their guest rooms and were getting ready to eat diner as Sid and his wife were preparing the boat and other camping gear for the trip to Kolcan and Copal Islands, Sid told to Professor Delgado that two British women were looking to rent a boat and some diving gear along with a metal detector to find sunken artifacts. Noticing what was going on, she told her husband that to get everything ready to leave in the morning before those British women might find the mask and selling it to the wrong hands to antique and ancient artifact collectors who would give the highest bids, Sid:

Don`t worry Monica love I`ll help you and the kids get to Kolcan and Copal Islands and find the mask before the bad guys try to get it, only they will get a couple of knuckle sandwiches and some wedgies ala barbie, after all your my wife and my kids who always love me their dad always give a good snorting adventure to have a good time.

Monica:
Oh thank you Sid querido, you're always be my huggy koala bear.

Sid:

Okay, let's hit the hay before we sail to the islands first thing after breakfast.

The next morning Svetlana was boating from the Thompson Beach Pier towards Pirate's Skull Island, there she tied her boat at the abandoned concrete pier, strolling at the pier to see if there was any artifacts that might be a clue that might indicate where mask is located before she leaves for the journey to Copal and Kolcan Islands, while she was doing that, she saw a strange shinny object of a Mayan figure on the bottom of the pier about twenty feet below the pier lying in the sand, there she decided to dive and retrieve the artifact.

Then she turns back to the boat to get her air tank and facemask and retrieve the shiny object. As she was getting ready to dive underwater when an orange arm slid out of the water and grabbed her by wrapping around twice the squid's tentacle around her waist to the chest by yanking her into the water as she screamed by seeing the giant squid ready to attack by using its parrot like beak to bite her chest and inject its venom to paralyze her as the squid drags down underwater as she tries to fight the cephalopod from drowning her and being devoured.

But Svetlana took out a knife and started to stab the tentacle by cutting it loose setting herself free, but the squid lunge itself towards her as Svetlana took out a laser gun from her pocket jeans and started to fire a laser blast when the squid wrapped on her with its beak open to bite her to death but she fired her gun zapping the squid's mouth and another with a death ray as the squid let's her loose by spraying her ink and swims away only to end up in the mouth of a sperm whale as his meal. Svetlana had to swim back to the surface to breathe and got out of the water to get her air tank and face mask and a plastic bag as she dived back to the bottom of the pier and picked the Mayan relic which resulted to be a golden mask; a priest mask which might have come from the Copal Island, there she swam to a Spanish sunken galleon by the name Galicia which took refuge only to be raided by pirates which in the end sank the Galicia to the bottom of the lagoon leaving any spoils of a pirate raid that went successful and to the Spanish kingdom very angry.

Svetlana got out of the water with part of her battleship blue safari jacket and her white jeans covered with blue ink from that fight to the death with the giant squid, but she dived back to recover the artifact and headed back to Thompson Beach to tell the others what she found.

There she told Annie and the professor on what she found and what clue might be on that golden mask that could be related to the original Mask of Colcocan, then her brother Gregory asks her on why she was wet and stained with blue ink.

Svetlana:
Because the squid was about to kill me and eat my lifeless body for breakfast if I didn`t zapped him with my death laser ray gun, I wouldn`t

be here talking to you and the only thing you be looking for is my skeleton lying on the ocean floor.

Gregory:

Gee I thought about asking that stupid question about having a near death experience.

Svetlana:

I almost had a near death experience if I had to zap that giant squid which his tentacle grabbed me from the pier and dragging me into the water almost ending up in his parrot beak as a breakfast morsel.

Annie:

Okay, but you should`ve told us that you were going to explore the island, that way we would explore it together.

Svetlana:

I know. I didn't wanted to get all of you getting scared but there was a lost map that I found in my room next to the bed last night and I decided to check the map before I went to be and saw an x marking on some sort treasure so I decided to go the island and investigate on where that mark was until I saw something shiny was reflecting under the pier when I decided to go back to the boat and get my diving gear when I felt something wrapping around my waist and I started to scream when the squid started to dragged me into the water and down under the pier where that giant squid about the size of me and started to snap its beak ready to bite me and injecting his venom to paralyze me to death when I took out my Bowie knife and started to stab and cut his tentacle so I could set myself free and swim to escape but it lunge at me wrapping me as he open his beak when I already took out my laser gun and zapped him in the muscle by his mouth and another one when he sprayed ink all over me as he escaped only to be bitten and crushed by a sperm whale ending as his breakfast while I got out of the water all wet and covered in blue ink as I went to the boat to get a net, my air tank and my face mask and dived back to retrieve the relic which was a golden mask lying on the bottom of the pier, but there was another artifact which was next to the mask which I retrieved and brought both artifacts so Professor Delgado-Foster could analyze both and see if those are authentic.

Professor Delgado-Foster:
Indeed they are, and these are not the only ones. According to the legend and the analogs of the Mayan Kingdom and the entire mask are named after each Mayan city or region that these powerful masks were created and they were twelve ancient cities: Chichen Itza, Bonampak, Tulum, Tikal, Colcocan, Cahal, Balamku, Sayil, Chacchoben, Xunantunich, Copal and Kolcan. These magical and powerful masks were created by the twelve powerful wizards of the Mayan Kingdom. By the way Svetlana; aren't you going to wash those stain clothes and take a shower?

Svetlana:
I better take these stain clothes to the laundry and wash them right away before the stains are permanent and take a good shower.

That early afternoon; Svetlana, Annie along with Professor Delgado-Foster and her husband Sid all went to Pirate's Skull Island to investigate Svetlana's discovery of that mask lying on the bottom of the pier, there they discovered by pier an ancient Mayan building of the size of a box square 2 story office building with drawings and hieroglyphs that mentions of the life on Mayan region and on the sea which has the Mayan calendar on the farming and harvest season, the rainy season and other events related to the region, then Annie found a strange golden chest on top of the table where a script was written in a leather contain vital information, especially of the twelve magical mask and the warnings about the powers if these twelve mask were aligned together if they fell on the wrong hands by unleashing its powerful magic force.

Professor Delgado-Foster:
We need to take this script back and translate it.

We need to know about this mask and the other eleven masks before someone else does. Svetlana; on the abandoned pier was there a sunken galleon in the sand bar?

Svetlana:
Yes, it's still there, but there's no treasure or other artifacts when I dived there.

Professor Delgado-Foster:
Later in the week, we will search on that island for possible artifacts that might have come out from both islands

Chapter4:

Sid:

Whoa love; does this means that mask might have fireworks in it?

Professor Delgado-Foster:

In deed they are; according the Mayan analogs, there was a league of Mayan Magicians who made and designed the twelve masks from each city that came from their origins and that each mask had its magic power when they meet at the Mayan city of Colcocan, the magicians headed to the temple inside a cenote where the mask were aligned in a circle in an island in the center of the cenote where the magicians chanted a phrase to activate and the mask activated their magical powers for peaceful purposes not for other evil purposes in conquering other civilizations or taking the whole Mayan kingdom under a dictatorship.

Later that night; Professor Delgado-Foster along with Cathy were analyzing the mask when they heard something outside the beach house, they went outside to check what was that noise, outside of the house were two shadows lurking in trying to burglarize the house. While Professor Delgado-Foster and Cathy were still outside, there was commotion inside the house especially in the studio room where the mask is being analyzed when someone was trying to take the mask when the burglar was confronted by Sid. The two slim fitted burglars lunged on Sid by using martial arts only to get punched by Sid's big hands and take one of the burglars by the sweater and throws the thief out the house and lands in the swimming pool while the second burglar is subdued and un-masked the burglar revealing the true identity which none other than Laura Craftshire while her Hench girl Heather gets out of the pool only to confront Annie as she lunge's at Heather as both ladies fell in to the deep of the swimming pool and started to have an underwater cat fight while Laura takes out a laser gun and fires at Sid knocking him out as he fells to the floor, then she turns to get the mask when the others came in to get the mask away from the tomb raider; knowing that she was surrounded, Laura decides to escape as Heather hits Annie as she gets out of the water as she tries to grab Heather by the foot only to see Heather take out her laser gun and zaps Annie as she sinks to the bottom as Gregory dives into the pool and swims back with Annie as both get out of the water as she regains consciousness seeing both women getting away empty handed without the mask or the notes as they headed back to the yacht.

Annie:
Looks like where not the only ones that knows about the mask and the Mayan city of Colcocan.

Sid:
Yeah like those two shelas knew about the mask and wanted to steal it.

Andy:

Like t aking photographs of the mask and the notes that Professor Delgado might have obtained from studying the mask and drawing figures.

Dwayne:

What are we going to do? They might find the other masks for a sinister plan.

Emily:

Those two thieves wanted to steal the mask and the hieroglyphic writings', well they took pictures of the wrong ones because Cathy took the pictures of the hieroglyphs and the mask and stored them in a secret vault in Professor Delgado's office, but some documents might have been compromised.

Annie:

It might be a good idea to sleep and investigate in the morning before we sail for Kolcan and Copal Islands in the afternoon.

The next morning as the group was finishing their breakfast and getting their camping and archeological gear ready in search of the eleven remaining mask that could solve the mystery and the riddle of the twelve masks of Colcocan and what was their function and use.

But back at the "English Beauty", Laura Craftshire and her sidekick Heather Leafshire were recovering after their failed attempt to steal the mask and some documents related to the Mayan city of Colcocan, but the tomb raider duo were regrouping their thoughts on what Professor Delgado and her crew were exploring on not only on the mask but on what.

Heather:

We were this close on taking that mask and some papers, but those brats got in our way and we were almost caught if I didn`t took out my laser gun and zapped that blonde girl as a distraction.

Laura:

At least we didn`t escaped empty handed, we got some notes about the mask of Colcocan, an according to the professor's notes, it says that there are twelve mask that were created for a purpose but what?

In deed what was the clue to discover the mystery of the twelve Mayan masks, but little that they know that their conversations were eavesdropped by "Don Bosco's" goons who went to Laura Craftshire's yacht to put hidden wireless microphones in certain areas.

Then they started to intercept their conversations when they heard about the raid on Professor Delgado-Foster's beach house to steal the mask that they found and the rumor that there are eleven other masks in the island. "Don Bosco":

We must find the map that will lead us to the other mask and let's not screw-up this operation or somebody will be sleeping with the sharks!

Both:

Yes sir.

Chapter 5:

Late that afternoon, Sid and his wife Professor Delgado-Foster and the group headed towards Kolcan and Copal Islands without knowing that they are being shadowed by two more ships about three miles apart without getting suspicion to the ones that are being followed to find the other masks as the other treasures.

By late afternoon, the expedition crews have reached the two islands; they started to set up camp not far from the ancient city where they are planning to search on both islands for the other eleven masks where legend says that the twelve masks might hold the key to something hidden that the Mayans build.

Near the island of Copal; "Don Bosco's" yacht "La Tintorera" had just anchored in the lagoon that serves as a refuge during storms and hurricanes; while anchored at the lagoon "Don Bosco" and his two minions were fishing when they saw two shadows diving in search of ancient objects that might lead to the eleven masks that could reveal the mystery of those mask and what function have to do.

Back at Kolcan Island; Sid was preparing his specialty dinner that he has made for everyone would love: Lobster a la Barbie and boy it's a great lobster with salsa, shrimp cocktail and Xochil Beth's favorite drink: pina colada.

Sid:
Good mates, tomorrow will have a great day as we explore the ancient cities of Colcocan and Mayacan in search of the mask. And by doing that we'll split in two groups so we can go on both islands one group on each island, and at the end of the day we'll be back at the beach camp for dinner and get some sleep, and speaking of sleep, it's time to hit the hay, so good night.

The next morning was a very important day because they were about to embark on a quest to search for the other eleven masks and what was its purpose, until Professor Delgado-Foster and Cathy Vlasco finally cracked the code on what was the mask function.

Cathy:
According to the scroll was that the twelve masks was used for peaceful used on operation of a quartz gyroscope telescope when the twelve masks are aligned together to the to the center of the twelve mask that will activate the trigger of the quartz by shooting a green beam to the sky at a starry night to search and identify the stars that haven`t been named by but have discovered and located at an early time.

Andy:
But comrade cousin; there is something that we don`t know about those masks and that telescope couldn't be used as a weapon to conquer other kingdoms and empires for military purposes?

Gregory:
What else is mentioned in the scroll?

Cathy:

I don`t know; but it will take some time to translate the scroll that Professor Delgado-Foster and I been doing for the last two months since we been web - chatting until you ask me that question Andy.

Cody:

Maybe those hieroglyphs on the scroll might have something to do about those masks if they had a blueprint of laser cannon that could shoot a ray of the speed of light that could destroy an object as far like the pyramid of Chichen Itza or the mask could be used as a gyroscope by using the amplifier to locate stars and different planets and to use the stars as a pattern guide for future season of planting and harvesting before and after the rainy season.

Professor Delgado-Foster:

Kids what you're saying about the mask maybe true, but we better get all our gear ready and split into two teams so we can search both islands and not one.

Guy:

But why both islands?

Professor Delgado-Foster:

The two intruders that tried to steal the mask that Svetlana found under the pier yesterday were trying to take my notes and a possible map on where the other masks are located along with the mask putting the expedition on compromise if the criminals get their hands on those masks.

Sid:

Then mates; let's eat breakfast and setup the teams and get ready to explore and find those masks.

After breakfast; Sid and his wife Professor Monica Delgado-Foster started to choose the kids on which team will join to, after the teams were formed on the following order:

For Professor Monica Delgado-Foster team.

Svetlana
Xochil Beth
Eddy Guy
Andy
Emily

For Sid's Team.

Annie
Cathy
Cody Manuel
Dwayne
Gregory

After the teams were formed, both teams received the same copies of the maps of the islands and the clues on where to find the masks and other artifacts that may be the puzzle in solving the mystery of the twelve masks of Colcocan.

Chapter: 6

Sid:

Okay mates; let's get our "duffies", camping gear and head to the pier as we sail for a "rutin snortin" adventure ahead of us.

Outside at the pier Annie, Svetlana and their cousins Emily and Cathy were waiting for the others as they prepare a second boat that will take them to Copal with Professor Delgado-Foster in search of the missing masks on the ancient city of Copal Kan where rumor says that the masks are hidden in an underwater cenote in a hidden tree trunk. Little that they know is someone is watching them from the bushes on every movement they make.

Regio:

Hey Gatula; look, there casting off to the island, we call the boss and follow them.

Gatula:

And what are we waiting for; let's follow them.

Heather:

That's what you think; have a zap nap, ahhhh!

Heather fires her laser gun but the two goons took out mirrors deflecting the ray and zapping back at her with devastating pain as she lays in the ground unconscious.

Regio:

Let's get out of here Gatula before the other tomb raider get us killed. Laura:

Too late; you may have zapped my Hench girl but I'll vaporize you two (Laura gets zapped in the back and falls to the floor) Ahhhh!

"Don Bosco":

What are two morons waiting for; let's go after the professor and those masks.

Both:

Yes sir!

As "Don Bosco" and his two goons run after the Professor and the kids leaving Laura and her hench girl Heather lying on the ground after both were zapped by their laser stun guns, three hours later as both tomb raiders have recovered consciousness after getting zapped from "Don Bosco" and his goons and now they have to get to the lost city of Colcocan before "Don Bosco" does.

At the Island of Colcocan; Sid and his wife Professor Monica Delgado-Foster had just docked at the wharf not far from the archeological site where rumors say that the mask might be hidden in the island's temples and other buildings and in the cenote in an underwater cavern where they throw sacrificed maidens and other enemy tribesmen from other regions. Later that night after dinner, the whole gang got together for the briefing before the two teams split, one to Copal Island and the second team remains in Kolcan Island as they search for the other masks and the telescope ray.

The next morning after breakfast; the two groups parted towards their destinations as one group headed towards Copal Island while the other stayed in Kolcan Island in search of the other masks that might be hidden in one of the temples or hidden in the cenote, or in the cavern of the lagoon.

Sid:

All right mates; now that the two teams have been assembled, where going to find the eleven masks that are hidden in both islands and where going to have to be careful if we ever encounter any bloody traps or any wild animal especially jaguars, boas and especially rumors say that there could an anaconda lurking in the waters but in the lagoon or in the cavern by the reef there could be a bull shark, a giant octopus or a giant squid looking for a meal and we might be the meal, so be careful. Now let's go after those masks. As Sid along with Annie Cathy, Cody Manuel, Dwayne

Gregory all walked towards the ancient city of Colcocan as they were searching towards the pyramids and the Great Temple of Rain and Fire while the other groups were searching in the other buildings when Cathy and Annie detected something in the old building on the basement below they found the second mask hidden in a sealed chamber thanks to a wide cracked hole on the sealed wall.

Noticing that the chamber might be booby-trapped in case someone tries to take the mask out of its pedestal causing the ceiling to cave in; they started carefully to take off brick by brick in order to avoid a possible cave-in.

After they took out all the bricks they saw more paintings and hieroglyphs on the wall but they have to very care because the floor may break apart and they will fall in to a pit that they wouldn't climb out especially around the pedestal where the mask unless the pit is full of water so someone has enough strength to swim out or otherwise drown.

Cathy went in to get the mask as she walked slowly and as she approached the pedestal as she put a small bag full of sand and carefully lifted the mask on one hand and lifted the sandbag on the pedestal with her left arm as she walks back toward the hallway with Annie as both girls leave the chamber without spurning a trap. But they didn't know that they were being followed by two female silhouettes shadowing from a far distance in order not open suspicion as they follow the two girls towards the main plaza where they rested for a while

On another pyramid temple called the Temple of the Sun and Moon also known as the Temple of Death; Sid along with his son Cody Manuel and Dwayne were in the temple in search of third mask of the twelve that they must find, as the trio were walking down into a ramp heading to an underground chamber which was rigged with booby traps before they reach the pedestal with the fourth mask which is surrounded by moat filled with quicksand.

Dwayne:
Ah Mr. Foster; how are we going to cross that moat of quick sand and get to the pedestal by removing the mask without triggering another booby trap and ending up sinking in the quicksand pit?

Cody Manuel:
Yeah dad; how are we going to retrieve the mask?

Sid:
Okay mates; bring me that crossbow and the grappling hook and I'll rope around the pillar and then I'll rappelled down the pedestal and lift the mask very carefully from the pedestal where I'll wheel back towards you two and get out of this temple the fast as we do before that rock comes down and flatten us like pancakes.

As Sid was preparing the crossbow and aimed at the pillar as he shoots and the grappling hook wraps around the pill and Sid climbs the pillar and glides towards the other pillar where he takes a rope and ties a knot and ties himself around his waist as he rappels down towards the pedestal as he starts sweating with nerves as he pulls out the mask and put's a small sand bag to avoid triggering the booby trap as he climbs back and glide back towards the boys as they unhook the grappling hook and swung back when it fell to the floor hitting a strange object as the three left the temple when the boulder fell rolling fast towards the moat and in to the quicksand where the floor started to sink with the pedestal to the bottom of the quicksand never to be seen again.

This time Sid, Dwayne and Cody Manuel were lucky to escape from a certain doom

Cody Manuel:
Boy that was a close one; we escaped from the clutches of doom.

Dwayne:
You can say that again.

Sid:
Now that we got the mask, I'm in a mood for a chicken jalapeño sandwich. Anybody is hungry for lunch?

Cody Manuel:
Yeah, but this time no jalapeños for me and Dwayne.

Dwayne:
I'll second that.

Sid:
Okay; wonder where are the girls, there supposed to meet us at the dock and eat lunch, okay let's go back at the dock they might be there by now

Cody Manuel:
There they are at the entrance of the ancient city, and they got the other mask.

Sid:

Good! Three down seven more to go. Come on let's go back to the boat and eat lunch, Hey where's Gregory? There you are, let's go eat lunch.

As the groups heads back to the boat, not far from there, the two amazon women who none other than professor Laura Craftshire and her assistant Heather Leafshire who were keeping close eye on Sid and his team waiting for the moment to capture the crew and force them to find the other mask on where that laser gun is. But another trio was watching them from behind and it was "Don Bosco" and his two goons who after the masks as the scroll on how to operate the laser telescope and using it as a weapon of mass destruction to conquer the Mayan region. On the island of Kolcan Where Professor Monica Delgado-Foster's group have reach the ancient city of Colcocan and the outskirt port by the lagoon, that's where they are heading towards the Water Temple where they use to hold sacrifices on a pure maiden to the rain god Huracan where they pray and ask for a prolong rainy so they have a prosperous farming on their crops and an excellent harvest when the rainy season has ended.

Professor Delgado-Foster:

Okay; we must split the team so we can search more wide ground. Somewhere around this cavern is a pathway or a waterway that may go to another temple called the temple of the Universe where the ancient astronomers studied and wrote down very important information about the star's movements and other information about the seasons and about the universe, the planets and other galaxies that influence the Mayan culture? The scrolls and records of the Mayan astronomy are written in hieroglyphs by using the masks as guides to locate a universe, a galaxy or a planet in which they might have discovered long before the renascence and the discovery of America by Christopher Columbus.

According to legend; the cavern is actually an astronomy laboratory where rumors say that there is a primitive telescope hidden in the temple that was built behind the cavern where there is a water storage tank that was built to collect from a spring waterfall in a cenote that supplies water throughout the ancient city that brought a lot of prosperity and peace among the ancient city but also to cool down the jade and quartz crystals that operated the telescope and the panel controls and primitive computers that might have been destroyed during the Spanish Conquista when the Spanish Conquistadors invaded the islands and rampage the ancient cities of Colcocan and Copal destroying the scrolls and all the science experiments but not all, most of the scrolls and science experiments hidden until this day, eighty years ago when the ancient Mayan cities of Copal and Colcocan were discovered by some of the islanders who were going fishing and crabbing when the Colonial officer heard about the discovery; they called archeologist and other museum curators of Great Britain and the United States and Mexico to search and investigate the ancient Mayan City of Colcocan and thirty years later the lost city of Copal was discovered when some fishermen went to fish on the lagoon of Copal Island when they discovered one of the temples covered in mangrove trees. The ancient city was cleared and cleaned in some of the buildings where there were a lot of fresco murals that are well preserved to this day.

Svetlana:
What a great story, but how are we going to find those masks? They could be hidden anywhere around the island.

Professor Delgado-Foster:
Then it's settled: You and Xochil Beth can go to the Universe temple by the lagoon, just be careful; some of the buildings may contain booby traps if we ever find those masks while Emily and Andy can search around the cenote area while I take Eddy with me in going to the other temple, be careful all of you.

All:
Right; let's go!

As the team started to go to their assigned areas in search of the remaining masks, three men were observing them from a hidden distance.

It was "Don Bosco" and his two goofy goons who want to get their hands on those masks and find the ancient telescope and use it as a weapon to conquer the Yucatan Peninsula and the World and eliminate their own enemies and nemesis so he could dominate the criminal world and the criminal underground.

"Don Bosco":
All right; it's time we start getting those masks from that archeologist and her helpers.

"Gatula":
But how are going to do that? One of her helpers might have saw us thanks to someone who always woos to get in love with some woman to date with. "Regio":

Hey! I need to find a lady who could fall in love with me.

"Gatula":
Yeah! Like you don`t know that any lady you tried to date with a federal agent, an American agent from the CIA, Naval Intelligence.

"Don Bosco":
Quiet you two or you're going to get us in trouble because of your yapping.

Both:
Yes Sir.

"Don Bosco":
Now this is what where going to do.

As "Don Bosco" was telling his goons about his plan, on Copal Island; Sid and his helpers were just finishing up his expedition on the recent discovery and the discovery on the three masks they found on the temples of the ancient city of Copal as he was about to report to his wife about the discovery when they all received a bad surprise.

Laura (with a gun at Sid's face):

I don`t think it's going to be necessary, now tell your team to put their hands on top of their heads or you'll have one less teammate.

Sid:

You won`t get away with it by taking the masks and sell it to next bidder!
Heather:

You are going to lead us to the next pyramid and find the other mask or you will be chum for the sharks!

Laura:

Patience Heather; we don`t want to have to mop the ground. Now where are the other mask and believe me Heather doesn`t have any patience.

Dwayne:

I will never tell you nothing! Not even a word of those mask at all!

Heather:

Yes you will or you be a menu for the crocs!

Annie (hits Heather with a right hook and a jab on the jaw knocking her out):

That's what you think!

And the fight had just started when Annie had lunge at Laura as both ladies had lunge themselves in the swampy bog as Heather had just recovered conscience and her stun gun and zaps Sid, but Cody Manuel, Cathy and Dwayne fought back as they all tackle Heather but fought back pinning both down as Heather gets her stun gun and fire's at Cathy missing her as she escapes from her attacker, but Heather fires back zapping Annie in the back as she get knock out cold only to sink under water as she floats unconscious in the bog as Laura orders Sid and others including Annie who gain back consciousness only to end up as prisoners as both amazons were escorting back to their yacht.

Laura:

Where's the girl?

Heather:

She escaped while I was fighting those two rowdies. You want me to find and capture her back to the yacht?

Laura:

Let the jungle take care of her, besides the sharks or the crocs will have her as their lunch or dinner. Now everybody starts walking to the beach and back to the yacht where we will head to Colcocan Island and get the other masks before my nemesis does.

Dwayne:

Who is your nemesis?

Heather:

Constantino Bosco.

Sid:

You mean "Don Bosco" the infamous crime boss of all the Yucatan Peninsula?

Laura:

Yes; the same that wears expensive suits and likes the finest beverage now move!

Things look as bleak from Sid's team as they are taken prisoners as their missing teammate escapes facing many dangers from snakes, crocodiles, and a giant octopus to giant carnivorous plants in some parts of the island that would eat natives and prisoners as a sacrificial ritual. But for Cathy escaping from being captured from Professor Laura Craftshire and her assistant Heather Leafshire was a narrow one but she must determine to find help to rescue her cousins and friends from sealing their fates in to the bottom of the sea in Davy Jones Locker for keeps but also alert Professor Delgado-Foster and the other team that they are in danger of being captured by the two tomb raiders and by the kingpin of Cancun. The big mistake and a fatal error that those two tomb raiding amazons was to go and destroy their camp and their radio communications which they forgot was an advantage to Cathy when she reached the camp to get on the boat's radio and alert Professor Delgado-Foster and the team that they were in danger and her team were taken captives as she manages to escape from them. There Cathy radioed them to get out of the ancient city only to cut off the radio when someone with a gun told her to shut the radio off and come with him otherwise she would see the last light when she is thrown to bottom of the sea to sleep with the sharks. It was Eulalio Tamez "El Regio" who was pointing a gun at the tween heroin forcing her to go with him to see his boss "Don Bosco", having no other choice but to go with without putting her life in danger as both boarded the goon's boat as they headed to Kolcan Island to meet Mr. "Big" himself in locating the rest of the mask and for the telescope.

Back in Kolcan Island Svetlana and Xochil Beth were in the Universe Temple near an abandon chamber where they found a clue of an ancient script about where the mask is as they headed to the telescope room there was another chamber with windows and a steel door and a hatch above the ceiling, without knowing that could be a trap, the two teenage girls went in knowing that the heavy door closed abruptly and the wall with a window closed shut as water was starting to fill in knowing that they are going to drown inside, but Svetlana is a good swimmer and a great scuba diver, so does Xochil Beth thanks to their parents in showing on to hold breathing underwater for certain amount of time, then both girls saw the hatch in the ceiling started to come loose as the whole door frame and the hatch gave way and fell hitting the water and laying on the floor as one of the stone bricks fell loose as it reveals the fourth mask as one of the girls would get it out of the next chamber as the water was filling up very fast as Xochil retrieves the mask and swims back as both chambers are fully flooded as both girls went up to the open hatch and got out of the water and headed to the other opening towards the lagoon by diving in the chamber and started swimming towards the surface of the lagoon as Svetlana and Xochil Beth reached the surface and swim towards the edge as the paused to rest before going back to meet Professor Delgado-Foster but a midsize figure with eight arms was lurking and was ready to grab and drag down one of the girls as they got out of the water when an orange tentacle reached out and grabbed Xochil Beth by the waste and dragged her down into the bottom of the lagoon as the octopus started to put two more tentacles Xochil Beth to constrict her and drown her by wrapping her in the mouth of its parrot beak and bite her by injecting venom to paralyzer her and drown her, then Svetlana dive's quickly to save her teammate from being the octopuses lunch as she took out her laser gun and stun the cephalopod by setting free Xochil Beth as she was about to go the bottom as Svetlana grabbed her by the shirt and started to swim back to the surface as both breathed air but the octopus tentacle grabbed Svetlana's right foot and dragged her down to her doom as two more tentacles started to constrict her by the chest and the other by wrapping both legs as cephalopod started to wrap her and open his beak to bite her by injecting venom to paralyze her and drown her as Svetlana makes a last ditch effort to save herself is to zap the octopus beak, but a second laser zaps her in the chest as the octopus drags the unconscious Svetlana out of the water chamber to his cavern as Xochil Beth dives back to the rescue and gets Svetlana's laser gun and gives the octopus a powerful zap that knocks him out as Xochil Beth grabs Svetlana and swims back to the surface as she tries to save the fallen heroin as she uses CPR to revive her as Svetlana throws out water from her mouth as she coughs and tries to breathe very slowly but stable as she thanks her for saving her life and she thanks for saving her as well.

For Xochil Beth this was first near death experience while Svetlana that was a very close second near death experience.

Xochil Beth:

Better rest and thank you for saving my life and you almost sacrificed your life for saving mine.

Svetlana:

You saved my life as well by risking yours.

Xochil Beth:

Now that we got the mask we better go back to see my mom and see if they found any of the other mask and here's your laser gun.

Svetlana:

The only way out is swimming out of the cavern lagoon and into the beach where we might swim to the camp and rest at the falls for a while.

Xochil Beth:

Okay let's swim out and I got your safari helmet, my kepi cap with the mask in the bag. As the two girls were swimming back to the camp, Eddy and Emily along with Eddy and Professor Delgado-Foster and Andy were going to the temple in search of the other mask, little they ignore that they were heading to a trap as the entering the temple, as they were heading towards the center of the temple when they find the eight masks already in their place as they encounter a jadebot firing laser jade rays as they saw a rat getting zapped turning it into a crystal jade rat statue. The only way to elude a jadebot without getting zapped an being turned in to a crystal jade human statue was to avoid making any loud noise as the four went walking silently as the jadebot was standing guard at the front door of the entrance then one of the jadebots spotted them as the four were caught off guard as the jadebot was ready to fire and turn them in to jade statues when the laser gun exploded destroying the jadebot in to pieces leaving only the crystal core of the laser gun that could be used at another laser gun, as they inspected the pieces and the core, they discovered that the jade bot not only it could fire a laser gun but their hands have copper disk in their palms to jolt their captors, intruders even their guards were armed with those jade rings they would aim and fire at their attacker's face or in a face in a hand to hand combat when the warrior pins him or her as they fall back an aims the ring at his or her face when the ring fires a ray at the face of the subdued enemy warrior and passes him out and then the fallen warrior is turned in to a crystal jade statue.

After inspecting the destroyed jadebot they all headed to the next chamber when another jadebot came in and started to get its laser eyes to zap at Professor Delgado-Foster, but she took out a mirror as the jadebot fired his ray only to be deflected back at the jadebot eyes as it started to short circuit itself as the jadebot explodes leaving only the legs standing as the mirror save's the professor's life. As they went in; they discovered the dome of the astronomy chamber where the telescope was housed not knowing that the main motor was under the temple that has the casings that fits all twelve masks that the main belt moves by rotating the mask as they reflect the holograms of the twelve mask appear when the jade light passes through the holes of the mask creating holograms in the night of the sky by trianglelating the stars and constellations in order to do their almanac based on the Mayan Calendar and on the recordings on the stars and constellations and on the sun and moon and on the other planets in our solar system.

Back on Copal Island; Cathy was trying to radio for help when she was stopped by one of "Don Bosco's" goons, as "El Regio" was forcing Cathy to board the boat as they were heading back to the yacht where "Don Bosco" was waiting to interrogate her, but there was a weakness in one of "Don Bosco's" goons which no one knows that one of them is an undercover agent with a good heart and would never hurt a victim but protect him or her if it was in danger. At the "La Tintorera" Cathy was being interrogated by "Don Bosco" on asking where are the other masks and the scrolls on how to operate the telescope.

"Don Bosco":
Tell me Ms. Vlasco; where are the other masks and the scrolls

Cathy:
I will never tell you about the masks and the scrolls!

Regio:
You better tell or something worst will come to you.

Cathy:
And if I don't want to tell you about where the mask and scrolls are!

"Don Bosco":
Then I am a mood for some shark fishing and you're the bait, bring her so I can tie her to the line, there I can throw her to the water; so the sharks can devour her.

Then Gatula heard what "Don Bosco" was about to do with her as he throws Cathy to the water as a triangular fin was swerving around as the girl is trying to avoid be bitten by the shark when Gatula saw the shark was about to kill Cathy, he took out his gun and shot the shark's head on killing it as it sank to the bottom of the reef where other sharks went in for the kill cannibalizing the dead shark's carcass like there were piranhas in a feeding frenzy as "Gatula" was plucking Cathy from the water all scared but shaken up from that near death experience.

Furious "Don Bosco" was angry at "Gatula", but he struck back saying to him to leave the girl alone saying that was a very cowardly act in putting the girl in danger by using her as bait for the sharks as he untied Cathy from the rope of the fishing line and giving her a towel so she could dry up.

Cathy:

Thank you for saving my life Mr. Gatula.

"Gatula":

You would do the same thing to me my little niece.

Cathy:

Uncle Gaby is that you?

"Gatula":

Shhhh! Please don't blow my cover, just do what I say or you put our lives in danger.

What Cathy didn`t know that the goon working for the big master crime boss was her uncle working undercover for the Interpol in trying to take down "Don Bosco" and his crime operation.

Then "Don Bosco called his two goons to bring the prisoner and get the boat ready as they were heading to Kolcan Island. As they were arriving at the beach "Gatula" saw something shinning under the sandy floor as "Don Bosco" told Cathy to dive and retrieve the shiny object, with no other choice she dived and swimmed down to retrieve the object was none other than the last mask to complete the set of all the twelve masks to operate the telescopic lens as they arrived at the beach when they saw Svetlana and Xochil Beth walking with another mask and were heading towards the ancient city when then they saw Constantino Bosco along with his two goons holding Cathy hostage, they knew if they make a false move they would hurt her if they didn't follow his instructions when "Don Bosco"

Knowing that they would get hurt; they handed over the mask and were ordered to accompany them to the ancient city without resistance or they will be killed at first site.

Then Cathy whispered to her cousin not to blow their uncle's cover or he might be put in danger too. As they were walking in the ancient city of Colcocan they saw the giant temple next to the lagoon where the jade telescope was hidden and the door entrance was open only to find eight of the twelve masks mounted on the power grid to run the telescope engine.

Back at the temple Professor Delgado-Foster and her helpers had just retrieved a key that opens the chamber where the telescope and the panel that operates it, as they observe; they notice that there are twelve casings with only eight masks in and they need the other four to fill the casings in order to operate when they are in the generator is on and the rotator with the mask is when it rotates by selecting the mask in its casing.

Then the mask is lifted to the chamber where its lock and loaded for the laser light to the three holes of the mask and the light travels through the open sky by creating a sky hologram, but the main purpose of the mask is to reflect the light by a set of mirrors that reflect the light coming from the laser and hitting it into the paper scroll to map and record the stars and new planets, each mask represents each month on the Mayan calendar which the twelve masks are used to locate stars and create an almanac that will show the season to plant and to season to harvest the crops, but one thing that the Mayan scientist main worry is that the mask and the telescope might be used for military purposes putting in danger the long lasting peace that has endured the Mayan kingdom for a couple of centuries.

Professor Delgado-Foster:
Now that we know about the history of the telescope, it's time to put the remaining masks and test the telescope and see if any of the mask is the month that we are now.

Emily:

But which one is the month of June and what mask represents the month of June?

Andy:

What about checking the scroll to see if the mask matches the month of June.

Eddy:

Your right comrade bro; if we check the mask and if matches the one that we have, then the mask matches the one of the scroll and from the place of origin and the month that represents.

Andy:

Exactly comrade cousin, there are twelve masks that represent the twelve ancient cities of the Mayan kingdom that are listed in the scroll.

Emily:

Which the mask is from the ancient city of Cahal and represents the month of June the sixth month of the Mayan calendar and the start of the rainy season, the Hurricane season and the solstice of summer.

Eddy:

We better tell the Professor that we better get the rest of the masks before (Eddy is interrupted by "Don Bosco") ....

"Don Bosco":

Before what? Before you tell the Professor? But I have the professor and your little sister and the other mask? Now where are the other masks? Or I will hurt your little sister and the professor?

Eddy:

Let go of my sister you tub of lard!

Chapter 7:

As "Don Bosco" and his two minions were approaching with the Professor and Cathy as captives; the others had no other choice but raise their hands and hand over the mask and the scrolls or they would hurt them.

The team had no other choice but to hand over the mask and the scrolls as their fates wait in front of the most notorious criminal of all Mexico and Central America. But little that they know that there was a hidden camera in one of the feather snake's eyes knowing that they were being watched; but who?

"Don Bosco":

As soon as I get the rest of the masks; then I Constantino Bosco will use this laser gun and conquer the Yucatan Peninsula and the rest of the American countries, and I will rule with an iron fist and eliminate on those will oppose me.

Laura:

Gloat what you want, because I will take over the masks and the laser gun and sell it to the highest bidder when I have finished with you and the others by turning all of you in crystal jade statues and put them in my secret submarine lair trophy room where I will put them in the pedestal mounts to preserve my victorious battle over "Don Bosco" and his clumsy minions. "Don Bosco":

I will resent that rant when I finish you and your sidekick and the others when I throw you in the cove so the octopus can eat you!

Heather:

That's what you think because Laura took the precaution to bring in our female bodyguards and they are amazons; lethal and dangerous, and now that we have the masks and the whole archeological site why don`t we bring in the prisoners.

Laura:

Bring in the prisoners along with the masks!

Sid:

Hey! Watch it! I'm not a punching bag!

Heather:

Quiet or I'll make a punching bag from your Hyde!

Laura:

Lower your temper Heather; now that we achieve our goal, it's time to test this ancient telescope to see if it works so that we can sell it to the highest bidder; now hand over the rest of those masks or I'll make Swiss cheese and pork chops from you Bosco. It seems that we are two people short and that that they have the other masks. Where are they?

Professor Delgado Foster:

I`ll never tell you even if might you feed me to the sharks!

Laura:

We'll see about that; Heather take some Amazons with you and bring those two girls and the masks! And now little girl, you will help me on deciphering the hieroglyphs on the scrolls or your friends will suffer by dispatching the first one to the coffin.

Cathy had no other choice but to do what the British Rogue archeologist or she would hurt any of her cousins, her friends and her brother knowing that she has their lives on the line.

Back in the cavern below the temple of Astronomy; Svetlana and Xochil Beth had gone back to the temple after swimming through the canal as they go in the water reservoir chamber when they saw the jadebots guarding the entrance to the telescope room, as they started to sneak in when they felt the presence of a steel metal on their backs as they were captured by the amazons and Heather who was gloating to her victory only to alert the jadebots as they fired their laser weapons and the amazons fired back hitting two jadebots the two heroines escaped to the chamber where the stone door closed shut and the water started to flood the chamber.

Back at the chamber where Heather and some of her amazons are battling the jadebots with the destruction of four of the bots as the other bots have zapped three of the amazons with death rays while the fourth had been zapped by one of the jadebots by pinning her down as the bot was ready to put aim of his petrifier ring directly at the doomed amazon's face as it fired a laser gun shooting a jade ray at her chest and the ring fired the jade ray directly in her face as she lies lifeless on the floor as she was turning into a glass jade statue as Heather sees the jadebot and shoots her assault rifle destroying the jadebot into a pile of junk as she rounded up the rest of her amazons not before another jadebot confronting another amazon in a hand to hand combat as the jadebot zaps the amazon in the face as she falls to the floor and turns into another jade glass statue while Heather escapes with some her amazons back to see Laura as the two girls escaped, but were trapped in the water tanks chamber that goes to the temple.

Xochil Beth:

It's kind of quiet and there's a lot of light through the ceiling in this chamber and there a lot of holes around these walls.

Svetlana:

This could be a water tower that goes to the radiator that cools down the telescope electric motor so it won`t overheat; besides it also goes to an aqueduct to the entire ancient city.

Xochil Beth:

The entire city?

Svetlana:

The entire city, look; there's a ledge and it might go in to the telescope room.

Xochil Beth:

What'll we do? The ledge is too high and there's an entrance above.

Svetlana:

Where going to have to float and swim to the ledge and then to the entrance to the telescope room with the masks.

Xochil Beth:

Looks like where going to get our clothes wet again.

Svetlana:

Yep, at least this is part of the adventure and we are very good swimmers and good divers.

As Svetlana checks the walls for a possible secret entrance by pushing the brick wall only the middle brick was losing enough only to her luck that water was coming out of the holes and one sprayed on her getting her jacket and part of her white jeans wet as the chamber was getting filled with water as it started to flood the bottom floor as the two girls, the water was reaching to their waist.

Svetlana:

Where going to have float and swim when the water reaches the ledge.

Xochil Beth:

Then we get out of the water and head to the telescope room.

Svetlana:
The sooner we float and maintain our selves swimming, we can get to the ledge.

Svetlana:
The water is rising; we better start floating and keep swimming until the water has reached the ledge.

Xochil Beth:

Okay, let's start floating and swimming.

Then Svetlana started to dive to the bottom as she started to swim the whole chamber in search for a secret door to go through the chamber and up to the telescope chamber where they have to meet Professor Delgado-Foster to hand over the last mask.Then she spotted a rectangular form in the wall as she started to push a brick on the wall and the rectangle in the wall was none other than a secret door that crumbled as it was showing another opening to a wet dock and an open surface appeared with direct sunlight as Svetlana surface back to breathe and get Xochil Beth as both dived and swim to the wet dock as both surfaced to breathe and swimmed to the wharf to rest before they climbed out of the water

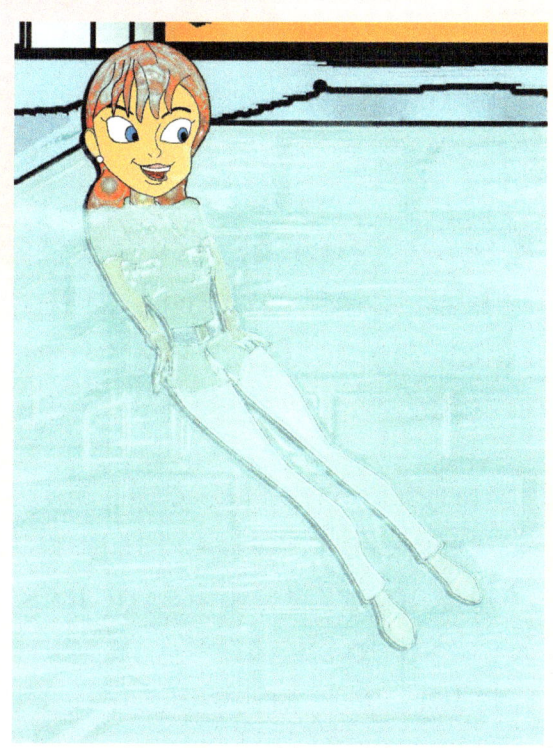

Svetlana:

Did you bring the mask?

Xochil Beth:

Not only the mask, but your safari pit helmet.

Svetlana:
Sweet; now let's get out of the water and dry up so we can give your mom the mask.

Heather (pointing a laser gun at Xochil Beth):
And to me or I'll make fritters to your friend and throw them to the sharks as an appetizer and you to the octopus as the main course; now move both of you and no gimmicks!

Back at the telescope chamber; the standoff continues as "Don Bosco" and his two goons as they were taken prisoners by Laura Craftshire's amazons as her Hench girl Heather Leafshire returns with the two prisoners and a few amazons that survived the confrontation of the jadebots while the others were not that lucky as they were converted into jade glass statues or they were zapped with a death ray and were thrown in to the water pit so the crocodiles could feast on the defeated victims, while some of them were taken prisoners and sent to a secret chamber where their fates were at the hands of their unknown captors whether they be sacrificed in a secret Mayan religious ceremony to be turned into glass jade statues and join the others in the hall of the sacrificed or to be vaporized in to ashes.

As they arrived in the telescope chamber; they noticed that Professor Craftshire had just finished putting all but one mask waiting to be mounted, as the last mask was mounted, the moment of truth was about to become the discovery of the century as she activates the telescope, then the mask ring starts to elevate as they start to spin until the light beam activates all twelve masks until the circle of mask stops spinning and the jade light from the telescope hits the main mirror and the masks reveal the map of the Yucatan peninsula and the twelve ancient Mayan cities and in the main observatory opens a portal door to another dimension of the kingdom Maya to be the surprise of some, this was no ordinary telescope but an ancient dimensional teleporter that opens other worlds including some related to the Mayan culture and other civilizations

Laura Craftshire:

This is no ancient telescope but an ancient dimensional teleporter and where there are ancient civilizations and ancient cultures to explore and conquer artifacts.

"Don Bosco":

And places to expand my criminal enterprise (takes out a gun) and to eliminate you along with the others. Now let's head to the portal and tell your tomb raiders to drop their weapons or your sidekick gets it.

Knowing that "Don Bosco" had Heather grabbed by the arm and his gun pointing at her as they all walked into the portal and headed to the wharf when suddenly; a group of Jaguar warriors started shooting arrows and spears missing them, but they fought back eliminating with their laser guns by zapping a small group as they retreated back to the portal as they tried to closed, it but it was too late, when Sid and the gang made a quick escape as they closed the portal and headed towards the main water tank that headed towards the lagoon and dived in to the tank swimming underwater that goes to the lagoon as they surfaced and swam back to the camp.

Back at the portal chamber where the fighting continued as the last of the amazon tomb raiders were being eliminated either by falling to the jaguar warriors by zapping them and using their petrifier rings turning them into glass jaded statues or by falling into a giant carnivorous Venus fly traps and ground man eating plants that grab their victims by the foot or by the waist, and drags its prey into his mouth closing it to digest its meal.

"Don Bosco" and his two goons manage to escape before the portal closed and so did Laura not before she saw her Hench girl Heather being taken down by the jaguar's warriors as the portal door was closed never to be seen again. Back at the camp the whole gang has reunited as they were trying to report and give all the photos and proof that the Mayans were indeed astronomers and scientist who were well advance in their time and by building the first advance telescope to see the stars and records other stars and planets and the movements of the sun and the moon on the season to plant and the harvest season, but there was more than that they found, Cathy found and took out of the portal the keys that operate the teleporter that opens the portal to the real ancient city of Copalkan as she had deciphered the last scroll of a secret lost city by the Mayan figures.

Chapter 8:

Annie:

Way to go Cathy you solved not only the masks of Colcocan but you discovered a secret ancient city that the Mayans have kept hidden after all these centuries that no archeologist has ever heard.

Professor Delgado-Foster:

But the keys that operate the portal must be kept in custody of the museum, and as a curator and director, the keys must be kept in a secret safe when we have to come back to Colcocan to explore and document all the artifacts that are hidden in this ancient city and in Copal as well.

Sid:

Than we had a great adventure not only taking down a crime boss but a rogue archeologist and her sidekick as well.

"Don Bosco" (with a laser gun):

That's what you think Mr. Jalapeno; now hand over the keys or your wife and her helper will get a one-way ticket to "Davy Jones Locker" Ahhhh!

Laura Craftshire (firing a laser gun zapping "Don Bosco" Falling in to the water.):

Have a nice zap and enjoy your stay in Mr. Jones Locker for keeps (Annie lunges at Laura Craftshire and both fall in the water) oof! (Splash!)!

As both ladies are fighting in an underwater hand to hand combat as Sid dives to rescue "Don Bosco" as he sinks fast to the bottom when he grabs him from the jacket and swims back to the surface with a defeated crime boss getting ready for the "big house" while up in the yacht "El Regio" is holding hostage at Professor Delgado-Foster and Cathy as Andy, Eddy, Gregory and Cody Manuel jumps at "El Regio" and everyone goes overboard in another underwater fight which "Gatula" took out his gun ad his badge identifying himself as an Interpol agent telling him to surrender as "El Regio" gave up as he gets out of the water as he puts the handcuffs at "Don Bosco" and "El Regio".

"Gatula":

Ah the catch of the day and its two big fish, thanks boys for your help.

All:

You're welcome Uncle Gaby!

Cathy:

Thanks for protecting me and saving us Uncle Gaby. Especially saving me from being shark lunch.

Agent Gabino Vasquez:

And thank you for protecting my cover; you're the best niece I would ever have (both hugging).

Agent Gabino Vasquez:

Constantino Bosco alias "Don Bosco" and Eulalio Tamez alias "El Regio"; Your both are under arrest under the charge of kidnapping, endangering a child and engaging in organized criminal enterprise.

But things were getting very critical as Laura Craftshire was trying to drag down Annie from trying resurface and breathe as Laura was resurfacing to breathe. That's when Svetlana ask her cousin Dwayne and her friend Xochil Beth to dive and get Annie to surface to breathe so did Professor Delgado Foster as she dived to help as Svetlana dives and swims fast to save her sister as she gets near Laura Craftshire and hits her with right hook to the jaw jolting her knocking her self-breathing apparatus as Annie is freed from the bear hug grip as Professor Delgado-Foster, her daughter Xochil Beth and Annie's cousin Dwayne swims and rescues Annie from drowning as Svetlana tries to swim away from Laura, but the tomb raider regain her strength and grabs Svetlana from the back of her jacket and grabs her laser gun and tries to stun her so she could drown, but it backfired as she tries to zap at Svetlana but the tables have turns as Svetlana twists Laura's right hand wrist and the laser gun fire's a ray zapping her as she drops the gun and Svetlana recovers her laser gun and swims away as an octopus appears and opens its self as an umbrella and wraps around Laura as the cephalopod bites her and injects its venom as bubbles come from the fallen archeologist screaming in pain as she is paralyzed and a tentacle is gripping around her neck and her waist as the octopus heads back in the cavern with the fallen and doomed tomb raider as its lunch.

Back at the ancient city of Copalkan there was a ceremony as they crowned a new queen and it was none other than Queen Heather who with some of her amazon guards started her reign as the Mayan queen to govern and reign to kingdom of the Mayan Civilization.

Will the portal to Copalkan be re-open, or it remain close so no one could enter or the natives could not go out and explore their ancient city again?

Back at the original camp; the teams gathered up with all the artifacts and other items collected as they were tagged, registered, cataloged and logged for the museum but the main problem was to take out the masks from the Universe Temple, and do the same procedure and the master keys to operate the portal to the ancient Mayan Civilizations and study the Mayan culture and the daily life they do in the kingdom, but it would have to wait for many years to come due to budget limits and other cutbacks on other expenses.

For Interpol Agent Gabino Vasquez; after hearing the report of the death of the infamous archeologist Professor Laura Craftshire eaten by an octopus, her arrest warrant was closed and her criminal cased record was sealed and marked deceased making the end of her criminal career as a professional thief and seller of stolen archeological goods around the world.

But the news of her accomplice Heather Leafshire whereabouts were unclear if she survived the combat against the Jaguar warriors is uncertain, but in his report suggest that she escaped with some of the Amazon bodyguards towards Central America, somewhere in Honduras.

As for Constantino Bosco alias Don Bosco and Eulalio Tamez "El Regio": both were sent to La Havre, Netherlands to face a lot of criminal charges from his criminal enterprise and would not get out of Prison for the rest of their lives.

Back at Thompson Beach, Annie and her sister Svetlana were finishing preparing dinner for the whole gang as they were preparing to celebrate the triumph quest of the discovery of the 12 masks of Colcocan and a new discovery of the ancient city of Copalkan that was never mention until now. Sid:

And now let's enjoy a great party and jump into the pool and take a selfie. As they all jumped in to the swimming pool with their clothes on, smiling as they took their selfie underwater.

The End.

Svetlana Kosakov

Annie Kosakov

Cathy Vlasco

Emily Vlasco

Xochil Beth and her twin brother **Cody Manuel Foster Delgado**

Professor Monica Delgado-Foster

Professor Monica Delgado-Foster, Cody
Manuel, and Xochil Beth

What a great adventure with all the intrigue, the suspense, and fighting the bad guys and a rogue archeologist and her Hench girl from trying to steal and sell to the highest buyer and bidders all the scrolls of the lost city of Colcocan where legend says that there are twelve masks would activate an ancient telescope more powerful than any modern telescope in the world which resulted in the discovery of an ancient portal that go from one world to another from that portal remains in the jurisdiction of Professor Delgado-Foster which will remain secret until the lost city of Colcocan is revealed.

Lightning Source UK Ltd.
Milton Keynes UK
UKOW07f0918250617

304040UK00009B/26/P